BRIAN
AND THE
VIKINGS

BY **CHRIS JUDGE** AND **MARK WICKHAM**

TO Senan
from :-

Sinly & Seamus

THE O'BRIEN PRESS
DUBLIN

About a thousand years ago, in a small village
in Ireland, there lived a boy named Brian.

Brian was the smallest
boy in the village ...

... but he was also the smartest.

Brian and his brothers loved nothing more than fishing in the river, hunting in the woods and playing warriors.

One morning they spotted a big, scary ship coming up the river.

VIKINGS!

'QUICK, we must warn the other villagers!' exclaimed Brian.

They ran back to the village as fast as they could.

The Vikings had spotted them from their ship!

'Looks like they haven't seen us!' snarled the Viking.

The villagers ran this way and that, panicking when they heard the Vikings were coming.

'I have a plan,' said Brian
giving each of his brothers a job.

Brian knew what Vikings
were most frightened of ...

The Vikings had landed and were making their way through the forest towards the village.

'Wait a minute ... that's no dragon.'

'After them!' yelled the Vikings.

But behind the rocks ...

'They're just leaves,'
snorted the Viking.

'That's no dragon. After them!' bellowed the Vikings.

Not long after ...

DRAGON CLAWS!

'That's no dragon!' snarled the Vikings.
'They're just toy boats.'

Around the corner ...

'Now **THAT'S** a dragon!'
croaked the Viking.

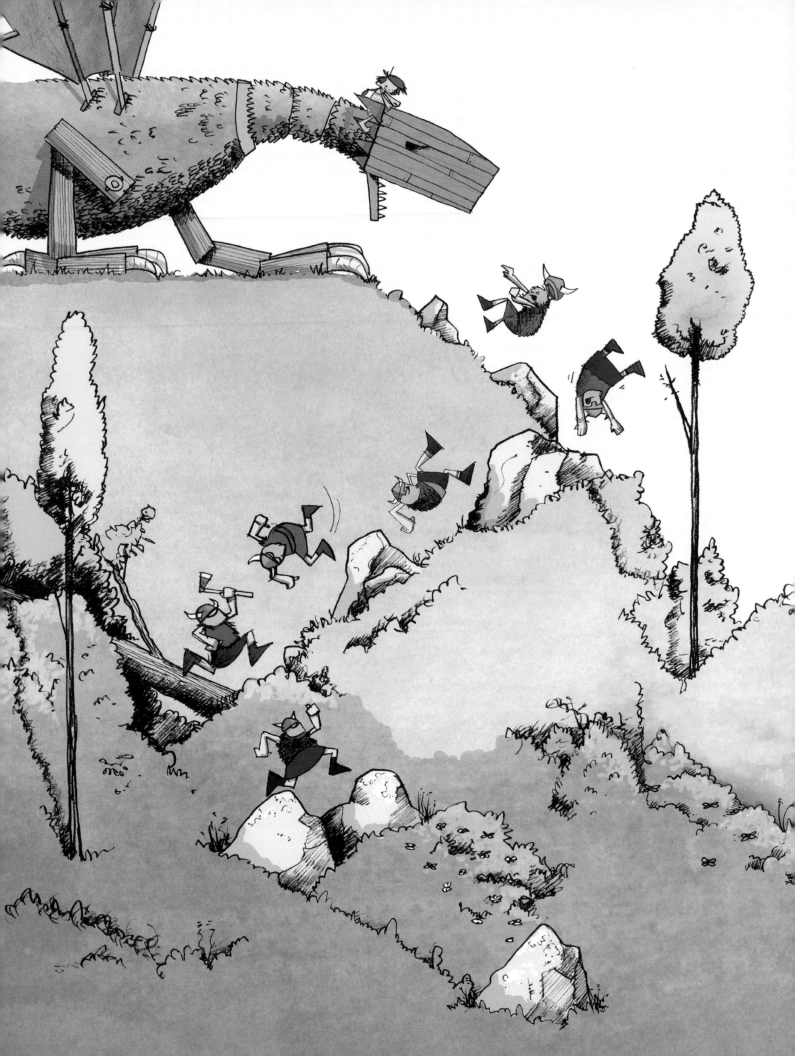

Brian and his brothers had used the fire, the leaves, the toy boats and lots of other bits and pieces to make a HUGE dragon. Brian launched it for its first flight.

The Vikings ran back to their ship in terror!

Brian swooped over the village and out to sea.

Brian had saved the village!

For now ...